JAN -- '04

To John Roe and Linden Days — K.G.
To Yvonne with love — M.M.

Henry Holt and Company, LLC
Publishers since 1866
115 West 18th Street
New York, New York 10011
www.henryholt.com

First published in the United States in 2003 by Henry Holt and Company, LLC
Originally published in Great Britain in 2003 by The Bodley Head, an imprint of Random House Children's Books
Distributed in Canada by H. B. Fenn and Company Ltd.

Library of Congress Cataloging-in-Publication Data
Gray, Kes.
Our Twitchy / Kes Gray ; illustrated by Mary McQuillan.
Summary: A little bunny named Twitchy discovers that there's something special about his family:
he was adopted by a cow and a horse.
[1. Adoption—Fiction. 2. Parent and child—Fiction. 3. Rabbits—Fiction.] I. McQuillan, Mary, ill. II. Title.
PZ7.G77928Ou 2003   [E]—dc21   2002155543

ISBN 0-8050-7454-6
First American Edition—2003
Printed in Singapore

3 5 7 9 10 8 6 4 2

Our Twitchy

Kes Gray and Mary McQuillan

Henry Holt and Company
NEW YORK

Twitchy was watching a butterfly being a butterfly.

"Mom," he asked, "why don't butterflies hop like I do?"

Milfoil smiled and answered, "Because they're butterflies."

"Pop," Twitchy asked Sedge, "why don't you and Mom hop like I do?"

Sedge looked at Milfoil. Milfoil looked at Sedge.

"Sit down, Twitchy," said Sedge. "There's something you need to understand."

Twitchy sat down and took a bite of his carrot.

"The reason we don't hop like you is . . .

. . . I'm not your Bunnymom," said Milfoil.
  "And I'm not your Bunnypop,"
said Sedge.

Twitchy twitched his nose and blinked.

Milfoil tried to explain. "Twitchy, your Bunnymom and Bunnypop brought you to us when you were very little. They couldn't look after you because they already had sixteen children to feed. They wanted someone to love and care for you properly, so we said we would, and we did, and we have ever since."

"I don't understand," whispered Twitchy. "If you're not my Bunnymom and Bunnypop, who are you?"

"I'm a cow," said Milfoil.

"And I'm a horse," said Sedge.

Twitchy blinked again. "But you can't be," he said. "Bunnies live in burrows. We live in a burrow." "It isn't really a burrow, Twitchy. It's an old train tunnel. We wanted it to be like a burrow," said Milfoil.

"But bunnies eat carrots all the time. We eat
carrots all the time," said Twitchy.

"It's very dark in the train tunnel, Twitchy,"
explained Sedge. "We eat carrots to help us see
in the dark."

"I still don't understand," said Twitchy.

"Come with us," said Milfoil and Sedge.

Twitchy followed Milfoil and Sedge down to the bank of the river.

"Look into the water, Twitchy. What do you see?" asked Milfoil.

Twitchy stared long and hard at the reflections in front of him. "I see two pairs of big brown eyes that always twinkle when they look at me. I see two great big kind smiles that always make me feel happy," said Twitchy.

"I see the two best bunnies in the world."

"But, Twitchy, look again," said Milfoil. "You have long floppy ears. We have much shorter ones."

"You have a white fluffy tail. We both have long dangly ones. Your fur is soft and gray. Ours is shiny and brown," said Sedge.

"I've never noticed before," whispered Twitchy.

He twitched his nose, burst into tears, and ran away. Away from the river, away from Milfoil and Sedge—as far as away would take him.

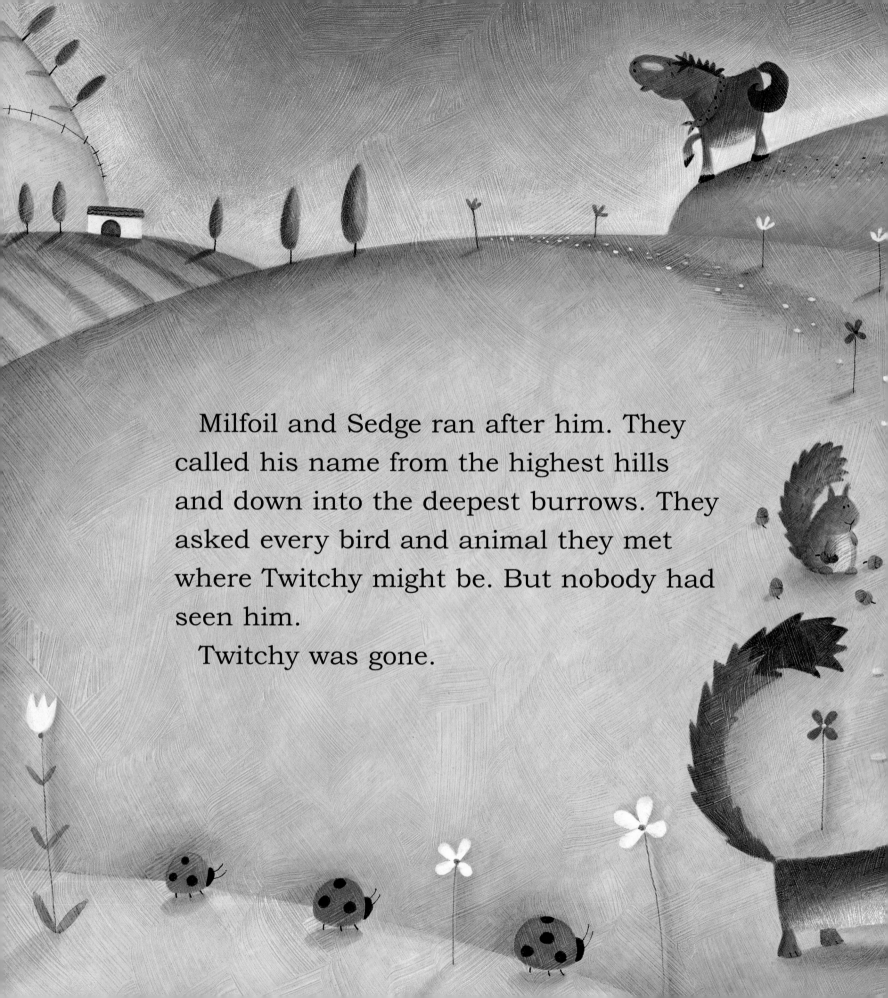

Milfoil and Sedge ran after him. They called his name from the highest hills and down into the deepest burrows. They asked every bird and animal they met where Twitchy might be. But nobody had seen him.

Twitchy was gone.

It began to get late, and it began to get dark, too dark to see. When Milfoil and Sedge started bumping into trees, they knew they would have to give up the search. Slowly, with big sighs and heavy hearts, they turned toward home.

They were two fields
away when suddenly Sedge
and Milfoil pricked up their
ears. A strange sound was coming
from the direction of the train tunnel. It
was faint and very trembly, like a "moo," or
was it a "neigh"? Milfoil and Sedge looked at
each other and galloped for home.

When they arrived at the train tunnel, they found a very strange creature sitting by the entrance. Its soft gray fur was smeared with brown mud. Its long floppy ears were rolled up and fastened with clothespins. It had a little dangly twig tied to its fluffy white tail. It had sorrowful little eyes and a twitchy little nose.

"Twitchy!" cried Milfoil and Sedge. "Where have you been?"

"Moo," whispered Twitchy. "Neigh." Twitchy's voice trembled. "I can change. I promise I can change. I can be a cow or a horse. But please be my real mom and pop."

Milfoil bent down and gently licked the brown mud from Twitchy's fur. Sedge carefully removed the clothespins from Twitchy's ears and the twig from Twitchy's tail.

"We ARE your real mom and pop, Twitchy," said Milfoil. "We've always been your real mom and pop. And you'll always be our Twitchy."

"We might not be bunnies, but we've always loved and cared for you just the same," said Sedge. "We don't want you to change!"

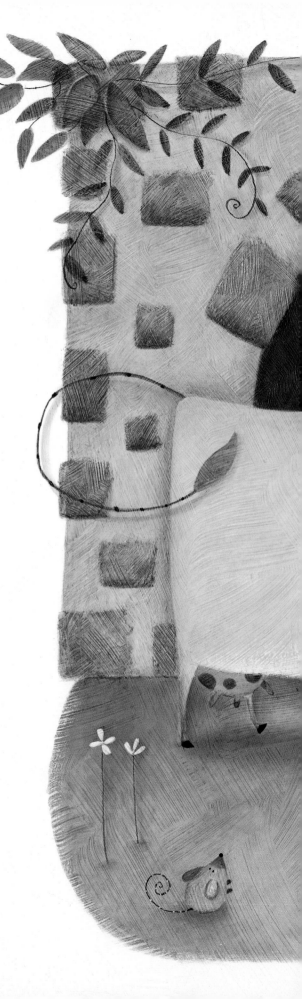

Twitchy twitched his nose and gave a little hop. "That'll do for me!" he said.

Ten more hops into the train tunnel, Twitchy turned and shouted at the top of his voice: "What's for supper, Mom and Pop? Mom and Pop? Mom and Pop?"

He liked the sound of his voice when it echoed inside the tunnel.

Milfoil and Sedge laughed and happily shouted back: "Carrots, son! Carrots, son! Carrots, son!"

They felt more like a family than ever before.